Neighbors with Benefits: First Impressions

Neighbors with Benefits, Volume 1

Paulina Young

Published by Paulina Young Publications, 2020.

NEIGHBORS WITH BENEFITS: FIRST IMPRESSIONS

First edition. May 19, 2020.

Written by Paulina Young.

Introduction

Paulina Young is a Best-Selling Erotica and Steamy Romance Author who is on a mission to spread positive vibes and love to as many people as possible. Hailing from the dangerous streets of south Chicago, she eventually escaped the mayhem through her storytelling and by venturing out to the suburbs. In addition to her passion for crafting romance-driven plots, she was crowned Local South Chicago Writers Club Author of the Year. Her various short story achievements also earned her a feature in the Chicago Tribune.

Before You Dive In!

Thank you for reading my book! Be sure to join my romance/erotica newsletter to never miss a new release.

Plus, I'll send you my newest book of my latest hot and steamy romance series for FREE of course!

Just click below to sign up for monthly FREE books and hugs from yours truly.

Click Here To Sign Up To Paulina's Sexy Newsletter[1]

---

1. https://BookHip.com/LVRGWC

CHAPTER 1 Unconventional First Impressions

It was raining heavily. Remy ran across the cramped parking lot, keys clasped in hand, towards her apartment building, her purse held over her head, barely shielding her eyes from the downpour. The streetlights blinked once; then she heard an explosion so loud that it could be heard over the roaring thunder. A transformer exploded. The streetlights went out.

It was dark now. The only illumination in the distance coming from the lighting of the apartment complex. Thank goodness for generators, she thought.

She tried to watch her step, but her foot slipped in a puddle, and she stumbled. But in her attempt to steady herself, she dropped her small purse and keys.

She tried to look for them but could only find her purse. It was too dark to keep searching. The rain was coming down harder than ever.

She finally reached her building. As she got on the elevator, she frantically dialed her roommate's cell number. Praying she would be home.

"Hey, Nicole. Babe, are you home? I dropped my keys and... you're not? When are you coming? Yeah, I know the traffic is awful right now. Yeah. No. It's okay. Stay indoors until the weather clears up. I'll ask one of our neighbors if I can stay with them for a while."

Just her luck. No one on their floor was home.

Except one.

She hadn't met the guy yet as he had only recently moved in.

She rang the doorbell. The door opened to reveal a 6 foot tall, nicely-built man in his late twenties, who had, judging by his wet hair, recently showered. His wet hair fell in dark locks down to his shoulders. Remy gulped. He was gorgeous.

He raised his eyebrows as if to question her. And she forced herself to snap out of it.

"Hi. I'm so sorry to disturb you like this. I'm Remy. I live next door." She pointed somewhere to the left.

Her apartment was to the right.

Her face heated up, and she prayed it wasn't apparent to him.

"Um. I dropped my keys when I ran through the rain from my car. This is really embarrassing, but no one else is home, and I. Well, my roommate isn't going to be here for a while...." She stumbled over her words, and she felt herself grow warm despite just stepping inside out of a full-blown storm.

God, Remy. Get it together.

"Hey, it's alright. Do you need to come in for a while?" He asked, then ushered her in. "Please. Come in. I'll get you a towel. I'm Callan, by the way."

"Thank you so much." She sighed in relief as she stepped inside the warm apartment. She noticed that he was still in the moving-in phase. There were boxes everywhere and save for a carpet, a couch, a table, and a few floor cushions in front of the fireplace; everything else seemed to be still packed.

He seemed to have read her mind because he mentioned it immediately.

"I'm still sort of moving in and haven't really gotten the time to unpack." He scratched his neck and smiled bashfully. "So, I'm sorry for the state of the place."

"Oh no, please don't be. I'm sorry for intruding in the first place." Remy waved her hands to reassure him. He smiled gratefully. His smile was kind of crooked, she noted. But that just added to his charm.

When he cleared his throat, she realized she'd been staring at his lips. She stepped back, ready to apologize, but he spoke first.

"I'll get you that towel."

"Yeah, thank you." She said as he turned away and went into one of the bedrooms. Remy mentally reprimanded herself and told herself to pull herself together.

He came back a few seconds later with the towel.

As she dried her hair, he went into the kitchen, and she heard him turn on the stove.

"Hey, you should sit down." He poked his head out of the kitchen door and pointed to the couch. "I'll get us something warm to drink."

"I'll get your couch dirty," she pointed out. Then an idea came to her. "Unless, um. Do you have a dryer I can use? And a spare shirt or something? I'm so sorry."

"Yeah, no problem." He waved it off and stepped out of the kitchen. "Of course, you can use my dryer."

Fifteen minutes later, with her clothes in the dryer and dressed in one of Callan's white sweatshirts that barely came down to mid-thigh, she was sitting in front of the fireplace, soaking up the warmth.

She felt much cozier now; she had been practically trembling and cold earlier.

"Here you go." Callan extended her a cup of something steaming, with a mismatched cup in his hand as he sat down next to her. She accepted it with a smile.

They sat in silence for a while.

She realized for the second time that night that she was staring at his lips. And for the second time that night, he cleared his throat. She quickly snapped up her eyes to meet his but found them staring at her lips instead. She gulped and unconsciously licked her lip and bit it.

She watched as his pupils dilated. She felt his gaze. It made her tingle all the down to her toes. Her heart was beating so fast she could feel it trying to burst out of her chest. Heat pooled in her belly and traveled to her nether regions. She pressed her thighs together to relieve some of the pressure.

Suddenly, watching him practically drooling, she felt a rush of confidence and arousal.

"Like what you see?" She smirked. She leaned in as he slowly lifted his gaze to look at her. She felt a feathery touch on her thigh that made her gasp as she broke eye contact. It was his fingers, lightly circling her left knee.

When she looked up, he was closer than he had been before. Too close. So close, she felt dizzy as she took in his scent.

"Is this alright?" He asked as his palm met her thigh, and he began to caress it, running his thumb in circles on the inside of it. His voice had dropped an octave. Remy shuddered with desire. She nodded weakly.

Their lips met in a warm, open-mouthed kiss. The rational part of Remy's mind was nagging at her to stop. She was being too impulsive. She didn't even know the guy's last name. She had never been with someone on a one-night stand before.

But she was throbbing, wet, and intoxicated with his scent. Their lips moved in sync as his hand traveled higher and higher up her inner thigh, and he started rubbing his thumb on her wetness through the thin fabric of her panties.

She gasped and deepened the kiss as she lifted her leg to climb on his lap, which he willingly allowed. His other hand lifted the sweatshirt, caressing the curve of her ass. Slowly, at first. And then grabbing it and letting his fingers massage her cheeks.

His thumb grew more insistent on her panties, and Remy whimpered into the kiss. He responded with a grunt and slipping his tongue into her mouth. She threw her head back as she moaned deep in her throat when he slid the fabric of her panties aside to rub her clit directly with his thumb, two fingers prodding at her entrance and then slipping in.

He pumped in and out of her, slowly at first, then he picked up his pace. Remy grabbed the hair at the back of his head and pulled, she then grabbed his shoulders and arched her back. She was panting as she felt herself nearing her edge.

Callan's mouth roamed her neck, nibbling on her skin lightly and then sucking on a sensitive spot just below her jawline, the sting sending sparks towards her groin. This whole thing was such a bad idea, but there was no way she was stopping now.

Remy realigned their mouths, pushing her tongue in and licking over his. She could hear him groan at the taste, the kiss becoming desperate.

"Callan." She sighed, in between hungry kisses. Her nerves were on fire, and she could feel herself tighten as he thrust in and out. "Callan. I'm so close."

Hearing those words, Callan removed his hand. Leaving her panting with her mouth hanging.

CHAPTER 2 Interruptions

What the hell? She looked at him incredulously. Before she could say anything, he roughly captured her mouth with his and flipped them over, so she was underneath him. She gasped into his mouth as he started mouthing her neck, biting and kissing. His hands moved up from her thighs to her waist and tugged off the sweatshirt. Breaking apart from her momentarily to remove it from over her head.

His mouth went back to work on her throat, nibbling lightly as he traveled further south, kissing both her breasts once, then moving down her torso.

Her hands pulled at his hair and clawed at his back through his shirt. He got up again to remove his shirt, and Remy admired him. He was certainly well-built.

His pecs were defined, and so were his abs. He had a happy trail that disappeared into his low-rise sweatpants. He returned to kissing her torso; she realized he liked it when she pulled his hair, judging by how his grunts became deeper and rougher when she did it.

He slid her panties off over her ankles and kissed the inside of her knees. Slowly moving up. Once he was at her entrance, he looked up to ask her for permission.

"May I?"

His voice had gotten even lower and rougher, and Remy all but came right then and there.

"Yes. Oh, god, Yes. Please." She begged. And he obliged all too eagerly.

His tongue was heaven and hell at the same time. She moaned and panted lightly. She wanted to scream, but she bit her tongue. Callan seemed to sense this and paused his movements to look up to her. She wanted to scream now.

Why did he keep stopping? He was driving her insane.

"Don't hold back." He shook his head and panted. His eyes were dark, and his lips were glossy from her wetness. "I want to hear you."

So, she didn't hold back. She whimpered and groaned and panted his name as his tongue slid into her and out again. She felt like she would pass out when he inserted two fingers into her and started pumping in and out quickly.

His fingers sliding in and out of her dripping wetness and his tongue rolling her clit were enough to send her over the edge. She came. Screaming his name.

Her legs felt like jelly as he helped her finish her orgasm. She saw stars in her vision.

Remy was no virgin, but she had never been pleased like this and never been taken care of like this. She had been with men who would wait until they orgasmed then pulled out.

"Wow." She sighed as she got up. Callan captured her lips with his and stroked her sides. She slid her tongue into his mouth as she sat up again, straddling his thigh. She wanted to return the favor.

She raked her nails down his chest and traced his abs with both her hands as he massaged her tongue. He was hard and throbbing when she fondled him through his sweatpants—and fuck; he wasn't wearing underwear!

She palmed him through the fabric earning a deep grunt from his throat.

He grabbed her wrist when her hands went to work at the waistband of his pants, and she looked up at him, curious.

"Are you sure? You don't have to." He looked so earnest, but he was panting. He was turned on. And she wanted to do this.

"I want to." She shook her head and undid the knot on his waistband, slipping her hand inside and finding his erection.

It was big and thick. It was throbbing, and her mouth watered at the sight. She felt a similar pulse in her groin.

She started working up and down his length with one hand, the other hand pulling at his hair as he crushed his mouth roughly against hers. They both moaned at the same time, arousing her further.

He started panting.

"That's right, baby." He grunted. "Just like that."

She removed her other hand from his hair and caressed his balls. This earned her a growl from him.

He was so vocal. It turned her on even more.

"I'm close, baby." His face scrunched up. It was the hottest thing she had ever seen. "Fuck, I'm gonna..."

He came all over her hand.

When he was finished, he looked at the mess he had made and grabbed the box of paper towels from the table.

He wiped himself and her hands. She looked at his face while he did it. When he looked up, she leaned in again for another kiss. They had barely touched their lips when her phone rang loudly, causing her to jump back.

She was confused at first, but her eyes frantically searched for her purse. She finally spotted it on the couch and stood up, stepping out of his arms.

"Hey, Nicole." She answered her roommate's call, trying to sound as casual as possible.

"Um, hey. Are you okay?" Nicole said. "You sound like you've been running."

"No, no. I'm alright. What's up?" She winced at her own lack of chill. Nicole would definitely bombard her with questions later on.

"Nothing's up. I'm coming home in five minutes. Where are you? You haven't answered any of my texts. I thought you fell asleep or something."

"Yeah. Something like that." She mumbled.

"What?" Nicole sounded suspicious. "Well, alright. I'll talk to you when I get there, I guess."

"Can't wait." Remy grimaced. "Drive safely."

Nicole hung up.

"Uh, your clothes are dry." She looked up to see Callan standing there. He had put his shirt back on, and he smiled at her. Her folded clothes in his hand.

Right. Her clothes.

"Thanks." She replied and took them. Now that they'd both come down from their high, the air filled with awkwardness. At least for her.

Callan looked fresh and relaxed.

"Yeah." She said. "Um, I'll go get changed. My roommate's almost home, and she has my keys and…"

She was rambling again.

"Yeah, I'm gonna go." She said and all but ran to his bedroom. His bedroom was as sparsely furnished as the living room. She hurriedly dressed and returned to the living room, ready to leave.

At the door, she turned to thank him again.

"Thank you so much." She smiled at him. "For everything."

He looked at her with a raised eyebrow and smiled before nodding and closing his door.

For EVERYTHING? Why did I have to say that? She thought. Did she just thank him for getting her off? She groaned with embarrassment.

"Remy!" The elevator pinged open, and her bright-blue-haired roommate ran to her. "I'm so sorry I'm late. The rain stopped literally ten minutes ago, and I rushed home. Have you been out here this whole time?"

"Hey. I'm alright." Remy returned her hug. "No, I went inside the neighbor's house."

"Him?" Nicole raised an eyebrow and pointed with her thumb as they walked to their shared apartment. "You know him?"

Kinda.

"No." She blurted. "I just asked him if I could use his dryer to dry my clothes."

Nicole turned the knob and stepped in, but not without looking over her shoulder suspiciously.

"Remy, you can't just go into a strange man's house and ask to use his dryer," she scolded her. "What did you wear while your clothes were drying?"

"No one else was home!" Remy defended herself. "I didn't have a choice. It was freezing! And it's not like I was naked. He let me borrow some clothes."

"What if he was a creep or something, Remy?" Nicole was exasperated.

"He wasn't! He was really nice. Stop worrying!" Remy hugged Nicole's side and tickled her. They fell onto the couch, laughing.

"Okay, okay, okay. Stop!" Nicole giggled.

"I'm older than you. Don't lecture me." Remy smacked her head when they sat up.

"By a whole six months. Sure." Nicole rolled her eyes.

"Have you eaten dinner?" Remy asked, standing up and ruffling her hair. She was getting hungry.

"Oh, I got you some pasta from work." Nicole's eyes lit up as she held up the plastic bag in her hand.

"What? I didn't see that before." Remy scratched her head.

"Yeah, being blind as usual." Nicole rolled her eyes, but there wasn't a bite in her voice. Remy knew she could be absent-minded, and Nicole did too. Remy often didn't notice things. She was forgetful a lot, but Nicole never made fun of her.

They ate dinner and went to their rooms to sleep. Remy had a photoshoot early the next day, and it was already late.

CHAPTER 3 An Attempt at Starting Over

At work the next day, Remy realized she wasn't wearing her mom's gold chain necklace.

"Where is it?" Her eyes widened. "Oh, no."

"Remy, look at the cameras," the director announced from behind the camera.

She was dressed in a purple silk jumpsuit and was shooting for a local jewelry brand. The director had asked her to look into the camera while touching the necklaces on her neck. She didn't remember taking it off for the shoot.

While running her hand over them, she didn't feel the familiar smooth, simple chain under her fingers.

She got back into her professional work mode, but her mind couldn't stop racing. She had taken it off yesterday but couldn't remember for the life of her where she had put it.

"Jasper, did you take off my golden chain before the shoot?" she asked the make-up artist when he approached her for touch-ups.

He frowned at her and replied, "No, honey. You weren't wearing a chain."

Oh no, she thought.

Just as Remy turned the knob to open the door, the doorbell rang. Remy opened the door wide and saw Callan standing there, his eyebrow raised.

"Wow, that was fast," he said.

"Yeah." Remy momentarily forgot what she had opened the door for, but then she shook her head. "Um. I was going to hang this outside."

She held up the flower wreath.

"Oh." Callan raised his eyebrows. "Anyway, I wasn't sure if this was your apartment. You forgot this the other day when you. Uh. When you came over. Must have fallen out of your purse or something?"

He held his palm open, and there it was; her gold chain. Remy almost fainted with relief.

"Oh my god. Thank you so much. I thought I'd lost it." Hastily hanging the wreath on the door, she took her chain from his hand and smiled at him. "I never take it off."

"Yeah. You're welcome."

"Do you wanna come inside?

"Sure."

She ran her hand across the side of her neck and pushed her lush, brandy-colored hair aside, revealing her pale, slender neck. She blindly fumbled with the clasp with both hands, gnawing on her bottom lip. Callan could see her protruding collarbones, and an image of their passionate encounter last night flashed into his head.

Her writhing under him while he bit and licked her soft, delicate skin. Barely holding himself back from marking it. He could almost feel her nails digging into his back, scratching down slowly. He became increasingly aware of the scratch marks on his back.

He opened his mouth to ask her if she needed help, but within another second, she was done.

She then tugged on the chain to make sure it was fastened correctly before smiling in self-satisfaction, her lip slightly red and peeling from where she had chewed on it.

Callan gulped. In broad daylight, she looked even sexier. Her lashes fluttered as she made eye contact with him and raised an eyebrow. Her smile faltered

"Um. Do you wanna come in?" She wrung her fingers together. She must have felt compelled to ask him that, he realized. He'd been staring.

"Sure."

He entered behind her, and he couldn't help but admire the curve of her ass as she walked in front of him. Her long legs seemed to go on forever. Callan noted that she was only a few inches shorter than him. Five-four, five-eight, maybe?

"Nicole, this is the new neighbor. His name's Callan," she announced as soon as they entered the living room. Callan looked around, confused. Who was she talking to?

"Hello." He heard a deep singsong voice from behind him; he whipped around to see a 5-foot-something, blue-haired, willowy girl who didn't look older than 20, dressed in a bright yellow hoodie and shorts. She was standing in the kitchen door with a glass of water in her hands and skepticism in her unusually dark eyes. He noticed that two of the fingers of the hand holding the glass were crooked.

"Uh. Hey." Callan didn't know why, but he felt like squirming under her gaze.

"You look familiar," Nicole stated as she tilted her head to one side.

"Oh? That's strange. I'm not sure we've met," Callan replied, maintaining eye contact.

Nicole shrugged and turned to Remy.

"Lia is going to be here in a while."

"Okay." Remy ruffled Nicole's hair fondly and led Callan to the kitchen.

"I'm not sure she likes me," Callan chuckled as Remy bent down to the fridge and retrieved a bottle of water. She turned to him, confused.

"Why'd you say that?" She poured him a glass while pointing to the round table in the center with three chairs surrounding it. "Sit down."

Callan took the glass of water from her hands and took a sip.

An awkward atmosphere filled the air. Remy was standing near the countertop, looking at anything but him, and fiddling with a dishtowel.

He took a deep breath. He didn't usually have a problem establishing boundaries in situations like this, but something about Remy made him cautious.

"About last night…"

"I wanted to say…"

They both started together and stopped.

"Go on," Callan encouraged her.

"I guess I was caught off guard," she continued as she made her way to him and leaned against the table, still not meeting his eyes. "I don't know what got into me. I'm sorry if I came on too strong."

"Well, it was certainly one hell of a first impression." Callan chuckled. Redness crept up her chest and her neck. She got embarrassed easily. "Wait, you weren't a virgin, were you?"

"No, I wasn't." She snapped her head up to meet his eyes, annoyance lacing her voice.

"Alright, geez. Don't get offended." He threw a hand up.

"Don't be an asshole," she scoffed and rolled her eyes.

"It's just a question." He put the glass of water on the table. "Calm down."

Apparently, he shouldn't have told her to calm down. She turned her body to face him; her face looked like she was about to give him a piece of her mind. What was she being so sensitive about, anyway?

But before she could say anything, her hand hit the glass perched on the edge of the table, and it fell. She managed to catch it, but the water had already spilled, all over Callan's thigh and splashed onto her shirt.

"Oh shit." He started to stand up, but Remy put a hand on his shoulder to sit him back down.

"Oh my gosh, I'm so sorry. Let me help you clean that up." Remy jumped back, opening a cabinet to get a towel.

Before he could protest or say he was alright, she was already wiping the water from his thigh. He wasn't sure how that would help. Still, he couldn't focus on it for too long because he was distracted by the palm of her hand right hand resting on his other knee. She was unknowingly applying a little pressure as she focused on wiping off his thigh, and didn't seem to realize what the pressure was doing to him.

"Remy, it's alright. Really," He said, his voice mildly strangled.

"No, no. I am so sorry. I don't look at what I'm doing, and I cause accidents like this."

His eyes dropped to where her shirt dipped down, and her cleavage was in full display. She had beautiful, big, rounded breasts. He felt a sudden surge in his groin, and a desire to cup them and stroke the creamy skin. To run his tongue down the valley between them and to bite and suck. A rapid image of her standing outside his door flashed in front of him.

Dripping wet, nipples poking through her shirt. The problem in his pants was growing evident.

"Seriously, it's alright," he emphasized and stood up. He had to make her stop.

She sighed and stood up with him, placing the towel on the table next to her. He tore his eyes from her chest, only to see her already looking at him.

More specifically, at the growing bulge in his pants. She looked at it with hooded eyes, her lips slightly parted, her gaze lifted slowly, and she locked eyes with him.

He gulped as she took a step forward and stroked his chest with her fingers.

One of her hands slid down from his chest to his abs. She lightly traced them with her hands before palming him right on his member. He let out a hiss.

"Your friends."

"Yeah?" She moaned. It drove him mad.

"Your friends." He repeated, huffing, as she pulled at his member. "Outside."

She retracted her hand; he suddenly felt annoyed.

"Yeah. You're right." She stepped back and pulled on the hem of her shirt. Then she picked up the glass from the table and walked towards the sink. "Close the door, then."

Was she asking him to leave? If she was, he couldn't really do anything about it. He was confused, annoyed, and mildly pissed off, but as he stepped out of the kitchen, he heard her call his name.

"What are you doing?" She asked, lifting an eyebrow as she perched herself on the now empty table, her smooth, tanned legs hanging down slightly parted. "I asked you to close the door, not to get out."

Without another word, he shut the door, turned the lock, took two strides and pried her legs apart roughly with his hands, crushing his mouth to hers. He dug his hands into her thighs as she ground against him, her mouth open, letting him devour her.

He bit her lip and sucked on it as his hands wandered from her thighs to her waist under her shirt. He slipped his tongue into her mouth, slowing down the pace and tasting her tongue.

He felt her smile into the kiss. But before he could ask her why, her hands moved from her sides and roughly grabbed his hair, pulling his head back.

The tugging pain on his scalp went straight to his groin, and his member twitched. She noticed.

"This is interesting." She smirked and then cleared her throat. "As much as I'm enjoying this. What is this?"

"What is what?" he panted. His head was clouded. Frankly, all he wanted to do was lay her down and fuck her into the table.

"What's your last name?" She asked after a pause.

"What?" He chuckled. "Really?"

"Well, yeah," she replied, removing her hand from his scalp and then caressing his neck a couple of times before letting her hands fall back at her sides.

"Price." He played with the hem of her shirt. "Yours?"

"Hunt. What do you do?"

He raised an eyebrow at her. She rolled her eyes.

"Doesn't this seem weird to you?" she asked. "I could have an STD or something."

"Well, do you?"

"No. Do you?"

"No! I get tested regularly."

"Good."

"Good?"

"Do you have a girlfriend?" She folded her arms in front of her, her pose guarded.

"What?" he sputtered. "No, Remy. I don't cheat."

"Okay. Good." She unfolded her arms and slowly put them back to her sides.

His erection had gone soft but wasn't entirely gone. He tried to step back from where he was slotted between her legs, but she pulled him back in.

He raised an eyebrow but leaned in anyway. Their lips met again. It was slow this time. Feather-light kisses. Like testing the waters. Which was ironic, considering how far they'd already gone.

"So, I don't usually do this," she whispered between kisses. Her hands were roaming over his chest and shoulders.

"Don't do what?" he asked, massaging her thighs, moving his lips in sync with hers.

"Hook up with people I've just met!" She chuckled. He hummed in response as he ground against her, producing a soft moan from her.

"Hook up with someone when anyone could walk in?" she added, nibbling on his lower lip. He hummed again, his hands moving up her shirt, tracing the outline of her bra.

"Guess we'll have to be really quiet, then," He agreed as he planted kisses and nibbles on her jaw, then on the curve of her neck. "Tell me what you want."

He slipped his thumb under her bra then slipped his hand in slowly. His index finger and thumb found her nipple. He started teasing it, while gently massaging her breast. Unhooking her bra with the other hand in a single go.

"Tell me." He ground against her once again while he sucked on a spot he had found last night that seemed to drive her crazy. He dipped his head down and then, using his hand, exposed the breast he was teasing so he could suck on her nipple. She chewed on her lip, trying to hold back her moans.

"I want to... Fuck!" She swore as he bit and sucked her nipple, circling it with his tongue.

"You want to fuck?" He chuckled as he looked up at her. In response, she reached one hand in between their legs, grabbed his erection through his jeans, and squeezed it. He cried out in pleasure, and she slapped her other hand on his mouth to stifle his cry.

"Be quiet now," she shushed him and removed her hand. He stared at her.

"You like to punish," he murmured.

"And you like to please," she retorted. "Is there a problem?"

"No," Callan smirked. "I think this is gonna work out just fine. I just wasn't expecting it."

Remy's face morphed from confidence to confusion.

"What do you mean?" She tilted her head.

"Well, you seem really nice and..."

"And?" She raised an eyebrow, but this was in curiosity—a completely different aura to how she was in a sexual setting.

"You're pretty and charming, but you're daring and charismatic in a more intimate setting. That's all," he remarked. Remy nodded.

Just then, the knob of the kitchen door turned, and they sprung apart. Nicole stepped in, their friend in tow.

Callan took one look at the friend and wanted to jump out of the kitchen window at the sight of the all-too-familiar Indian girl. She gasped when she met his eyes.

"Callan?" She all but shouted.

"Alia." He said. Fuck. What was she doing here? Was she their friend?

"You two know each other?" Remy was red in the face as she unsuccessfully tried to fix her clothing.

"How do you know him?" Alia turned to Remy, tears in her eyes. Oh, god, no.

"Um, he's my new neighbor," Remy explained, frantic. "What's wrong?"

"I think you should leave." Nicole's melodic voice cut through the strained atmosphere. She was looking at him with the same skeptical gaze.

"See you around." He waved to Remy and cut past Alia as fast as he could. He had no desire to stick around for an Alia tantrum. He'd seen enough of them when they were sort-of dating.

He sprinted out of their apartment and into his. Fuck. The world just had to be this fucking small.

CHAPTER 4 Making Better Decisions

Alia sobbed as she sat on the kitchen table as Remy caressed her thick black hair.

"I knew I'd seen him from somewhere," Nicole stated as she stood in the doorway, looking at Alia with softness in her eyes. "I saw his pictures in Lia's gallery."

"He's my ex-boyfriend." Alia wiped her tears.

"What happened?" Remy bit her lip. She hated seeing her friend cry, but she was curious. She needed to know about Callan. Especially after what they'd done. Oh god. This was exactly why she didn't do it with strangers.

"Remy, he's a liar." Alia looked into Remy's eyes. "He's really sweet and charming in person and makes you feel like you're the only one he sees, and then he flips the switch."

"What do you mean?"

"We dated for three months last year when I interned at his dad's company. He's so caring at first but then. Remy, he's like, obsessed with his work. He told me not to tell anyone at work, so I didn't. He has a million personalities. He used to ignore me for days and then come to my apartment and act like nothing even happened. When I asked him, he used to get cold and distant. He dumped me with a phone call, and a few days later, I caught him making out with a temp in the copy room. He was obviously cheating on me." Alia broke down again.

"Oh, sweetie. I had no idea." Remy soothed her friend and rubbed circles on her back. She felt a surge of anger towards Callan. "What a jerk."

"I quit the next day. I just couldn't take it anymore."

"I understand, sweetie." Remy consoled her. Callan had seemed like such a charming, easygoing guy.

Remy figured she shouldn't really be judging people at first encounters anymore. She'd only met the guy twice, and they'd spent half the time trying to fuck. She decided she would stay more alert. She knew she could be absent-minded and a klutz, but she wasn't stupid.

Callan hit the pedal as soon as he saw another car aiming for the same parking spot as him. It was a dingy old Ford, and the sun was hitting its windshield at an angle so he couldn't see who was in the driver's seat. It didn't really matter to him, anyway. He got the spot and stepped out of the car, taking off his sunglasses in one swift motion.

As he stepped into the elevator to his apartment and the door was closing, he saw Remy running towards him. He stopped the elevator by putting his foot between the closing doors.

She stepped in, and the doors closed.

She turned around and glared at him, which he returned with a confused look of his own.

"Aren't you supposed to say thank you? What'd I do?"

"You stole my parking spot." She scoffed.

"That was you?" He chuckled. "Oops."

She wasn't amused. Oops.

CHAPTER 5 Here We Go Again

Five minutes later, they stumbled into his bedroom, hands grabbing at each other, lips locked in a clumsy yet heated kiss. Callan guided her to his bed and lay her down as he started devouring her neck.

Remy felt a familiar heat pool in her abdomen as his fingers went under her skirt and between her legs, rubbing her clit.

"Tell me what you want," he panted as he lifted his head to ask before crushing her lips with his. The gears in her mind ground to a halt.

"Alia told me about you," she said instead.

"Did she?" He said nonchalantly, as he continued to prod at her entrance, slipping one finger inside. Remy moaned in pleasure.

"Ah. Callan. Callan, stop." Remy grabbed his wrist. He stopped immediately, and she sat back up.

"You cheated on her," she said accusingly.

"I did not cheat on her, Remy." His gaze turned dark, and his voice, serious.

"Yeah? Then who were you making out with in the copy room, three days after you dumped her?"

He threw his hands in the air and sighed.

"If that's what you are going to think based on Alia's perspective only, then that's your own choice, I guess." He rolled his eyes.

Remy scoffed.

"I didn't cheat on her, okay? Alia and I were never exclusive in the first place. I agree," Callan sat back and rubbed a hand over his face. "I may have been a jerk about it, but I had my reasons, and you're being biased, so whatever, I guess. I don't do commitments, Remy. I have more important things to do. Alia knew that. So, I am just going to say it."

"Say what?" She folded her arms in front of her.

He crawled back to her and got within an inch of her face. Remy looked him in the eye, unwavering, but the pressure between her legs returned. God, he shouldn't get her all riled up just by coming close to her.

"I find you very attractive." His voice dropped an octave as he said it. Remy gulped and pushed her thighs together as her mind raced. How she wanted to push him down and have those lips work on her pussy! He came closer and stopped within a millimeter of her lips, she leaned forward but as soon as he touched them, she pulled back.

"But if you're going to get angry and jealous every time I hook up with someone else, then I guess there's no point in having this conversation." He stepped back from the bed and grabbed a towel that was draped on the back of a chair. "We can go back to being strangers. Which shouldn't be a problem, since we already are."

He turned his back to her and opened the door to the bathroom, closing it behind him. Remy was still sitting there, half aroused and half infuriated. Did he just leave her there after getting her all worked up like that? She was in a dilemma. She wasn't particularly attached to Callan. Sure, he had made her feel so fucking good, but he could keep doing that. She just had to be careful and not fall for him.

As she heard the shower running, an idea came to her.

Five minutes later, Callan stepped out of the shower, towel hanging low on his hips as he dried his hair with a white cotton shirt.

He stopped in his tracks as soon as his eyes fell on her. She quite relished how wide and dark his eyes got as he took her in, sprawled on his bed in nothing but her bra and panties. He opened and closed his mouth a few times.

"Close your mouth, sweetie." She grinned as he obeyed.

"You're still here."

"Excellent observation."

"That means..."

"That means I agree. I won't get jealous. You can do what you want." She shrugged. "Now, come here."

He took a few tentative steps towards the bed, and as soon as he reached it, she leaned up to capture his lips with her own, lifting herself to straddle him. He raised his hands to slide them up her thighs. He seemed to have a thing for her legs.

"I didn't say you could touch me." She grabbed his hair. "You're not allowed to touch me until I tell you."

"Okay."

"Lie down, won't you?" She pushed back his shoulders until he lay on his back, hands clenched at his sides. She kissed him again, slowly this time. She dipped her tongue in his mouth, and their tongues danced. She then took his tongue between her teeth and sucked, producing a groan deep from his throat.

She moved her lips down to his neck, then to his broad, muscular chest, nibbling, biting, and sucking until she reached his nipples. He bit his lip to stifle his groan as she licked his left nipple.

"I know for a fact you can get much louder than that. Don't hold back." She caressed his face.

"Fuck. Remy." He groaned even louder.

"Does that feel good?" She rubbed his nipple with the tip of her tongue. On the inside of her thigh, she felt his member twitch. She smiled at him.

"Yes. Fuck, that feels good."

She ground her hip hard against his erection, surprising him. His hands shot up, and she pushed them back, earning a glare from him.

"What did I tell you?" She reprimanded with a smile as she moved in a motion that caused her inner thigh to rub against his towel-covered member.

Using her hand, she freed him of the towel. His cock sprang out. God, he was big. Remy's mouth watered as she ran her fingers down his shaft, making him twitch.

"You're so hard already." She grabbed his member and squeezed lightly.

A string of curses left Callan's mouth.

"Fuck, Remy. Come on."

"Tell me what you want." She replied, echoing his earlier words. He narrowed his eyes at her.

"I want." He started slowly. "I want you."

"You want me to what, Callan?" She tilted her head. "Say it."

"I want to fuck you. Fuck, Remy." He growled as she squeezed his shaft again. He bucked up his hips, digging his fingers into the mattress. "I want to touch you."

"Ask nicely." Remy was just having fun now. But seeing his state. The veins on his neck were bulging. His face, neck, and chest were red and sweaty. She knew it would be worth it.

"Remy. Please let me fuck you." He said each word in between gasps.

"Then do it."

She didn't have to ask him twice. Within one swift motion, he had her under him. His hands were roaming her body like it was something he needed to do to survive. With a fervor that a traveler would feel after seeing an oasis in the middle of a week's journey into the Sahara. He sucked on her neck, on her collarbones, on her breasts and had her panting and moaning his name.

With a trembling hand, he slipped off her panties and filled her with his length. Remy's eyes closed in bliss, and she saw stars as he filled her to the brim in one go. She had been soaking wet already. He pulled out slowly and went in again.

She lifted her legs and hooked them over his shoulders for better access.

He hit her sweet spot with one swift stroke. Remy moaned and dug her nails into his back.

"You have no idea," Callan panted, "how much I've wanted to do that ever since I first saw you."

"Go faster." She gasped. "Right there, Callan."

Callan was good. In fact, Remy didn't remember it ever being this good. Somewhere in between thrusts, Callan's thumb found its way to her clit and rubbed it. Her mind almost short-circuited.

With a few final well-placed thrusts, Remy came. Her back arched as waves of pleasure overcame her body and her senses. Callan pulled out, and as soon as Remy came down from her high, she pushed him back with wobbly arms and took his erection in her mouth. It didn't take him long to release, and she lapped up his cum as much as she could.

He grabbed her face gently and brought her up to look at him. His cum was dripping down her cheeks. He kissed her gently as he got up and retrieved a box of paper towels from the nightstand to clean her face.

He cleaned her up with one hand and caressed her face with the other. Then he got up and took her into the shower.

"Do you wanna take a shower?" he asked, kissing her neck. Remy hummed and nodded. She had just had the best sex of her life. Her mind was in a haze, and she felt sleepy.

"Yeah, I'll clean up." She opened the tap and rinsed her mouth.

Callan chuckled and ruffled her hair one last time before closing the door and leaving her by herself.

CHAPTER 6
MISTAKES IN AFTERCARE

"I made a quick pasta," Callan announced as soon as he saw Remy step into the kitchen, her hair dripping wet and her eyes wide. She looked innocent and ethereal. Not at all like the woman that had dominated him in the bedroom. Her duality was enticing yet endearing.

"Oh." She yawned as she took a seat. "You can cook?"

"Why are you surprised?" He cocked an eyebrow.

"Well, your apartment is a mess." She waved her hand around. "You don't seem like the domestic type."

He smiled.

"Wow, this is good." Remy's eyes widened as she chewed on a bite of cheesy pasta. "There are so many flavors in this."

"You're welcome." His chest swelled.

"How is this a quick pasta?" She air-quoted. "You could totally be a chef if you weren't a business geek."

"I am not a business geek." He rolled his eyes. But he felt defensive. He didn't know why, maybe because being a chef was something he did want to do. But it was too late for that. He was an heir, and his parents had never approved of his culinary interests. Nevertheless, it struck a nerve. "It's just not something I can pursue."

"Why not?" She persisted. "If it's something you want to do, then you should."

He started to squirm.

"Let it go." It came out harsher than he had intended, and Remy seemed to have picked up on it. She put her fork down and reached out her hand to stroke his arm.

"Hey," she said, "I'm just saying..."

"Remy, fucking drop it. Yeah?"

She dropped her hand and looked down. A beat later, she got up from her seat. Callan felt a wave of anger at her empathy. He shouldn't have felt like that, but he did. He had known her for only a week. Why was she looking at him like she could see through his walls?

He remembered earlier when she had looked questioningly at the burn scars on his shoulder. A vivid memory of burned cigarette stubs being pressed into his skin, seared his brain. It went away as quickly as it came, but he didn't realize he had cried out because Remy was in front of him, holding his face and looking at him with those big green eyes of hers.

"Callan, are you okay?"

"Get out." He spat. "You don't know shit about my life."

"I never said I did."

Callan snarled.

"Then stop with the sympathy. What do you even know? You're a model. All you had to do was rely on your looks your whole life."

The next few seconds passed by in a blur. Callan felt the sharp sting of a slap on his face. Then heard his door bang shut.

A week passed. Remy went to work every day, came home, ate, went to sleep, and went to work again.

She felt low and horrible about what Callan had said to her. And she was tired of people assuming stuff like that about her.

She worked hard at whatever she did. She studied acting in college, and she always did her research about her modeling gigs. It pissed her off when someone assumed she had always had it easy. Or was stupid.

One night, Alia noticed her sulking under the blankets and offered to take her out.

"Come on! We're going to have fun," she said, "we'll dance, and maybe you will meet a cute guy. Come on!"

She tried tugging the blanket off. But Remy held on to it and whimpered in protest.

"I'll do your makeup. Where's that red dress that we got the other day?"

"I am really not in the mood, Lia."

"Why not? You're always in the mood for dancing."

"Not tonight," Remy mumbled.

"Did something happen?" Lia sat on the edge of her bed and asked. Then she paused and added, "Is it Callan?"

Remy stiffened under the blanket.

"Are you mad at me?" She poked her head out of the blanket and asked Lia.

"No, you idiot. Tell me what happened."

Remy took a deep breath and did what Lia asked.

CHAPTER 7
TOO GOOD

Callan's doorbell rang, he opened the door to see Alia standing there, all dressed up and obviously ready to go out.

He raised an eyebrow. "What are you doing here?"

"I need to talk to you before I leave. I'll only take five minutes," Alia replied with a stony expression on her face.

"Okay." He ran a hand through his hair. "What's up?"

Alia began, "I know you don't have any feelings whatsoever and are a cold-hearted bastard. But don't mess with my friend."

"I didn't mess with your friend," he sputtered furiously.

"Yeah, you did."

"Look, I didn't mean it, okay?"

"Whatever, Callan. Remy isn't someone you can play with, okay? She's a good person."

"I know that," he mocked. "Anything else?"

"Lia, hurry up!" He heard Nicole's voice call from where the elevators were. But his eyes were fixed on Alia.

"Get your act together. I know you have issues with your parents. The whole company knew it when I worked there, okay? If you're too much of a coward to stand up to your parents, don't take it out on my friend."

"Are you done?" He gritted his teeth together; he was seconds away from shutting the door in her face.

"Yeah, so get your act together," she told him.

"Goodbye, Alia." He slammed the door in her face. It felt satisfying, but his heart was racing. He ran a hand through his hair and down his face as he sank down with his back to the front door.

Callan went to the shooting site the other day a little late. He hadn't gotten a good night's sleep.

He arrived to see the shooting was already in progress. Remy was listening to the director's instructions, frowning and nodding, giving her own input from time to time.

From the corner of his eye, he saw a lanky spot boy drag an unstable-looking ladder over so he could adjust the tall lights. He climbed up it when the director cued them to start.

Callan saw Remy's whole aura change to work according to their concept. Her expressions, her posture, everything exuded confidence and self-assurance. She was a professional, and Callan couldn't help but admire her.

He heard something snap and then a jolt. He turned quickly to see the ladder falling down. Dropping right onto the flimsy backdrop, causing it to collapse. He only saw the brief look of surprise on Remy's face before she disappeared under the mess.

"Remy!" he called, rushing over to help her out. She had been knocked from the stool she was sitting on, and she was pushing away the backdrop with one hand, wincing.

She peeked from beneath it. "Callan?"

"You alright? Didn't hit your head or anything?"

"No." She sat up. "What are you doing here?"

"I'm overseeing this project." He knelt beside her and reached out to touch her, just to examine her, but she batted his hand away.

"I'm fine," she asserted.

"Oh." A feeling of smallness crept over him at the annoyance in her voice. He stood and stuffed his hands in his pockets. "If you're fine, come with me to get a coffee? I don't know anyone here, and it's lunch break in five minutes."

She assessed the mess around her as she looked at him with a strange look on her face. "I want to tidy up; I'm not hungry. You go ahead."

"Right. Um." He scratched the back of his neck. "You sure you don't need any help?" He offered his hand, and she studied it for a moment before she pulled on it. And for whatever reason, be it his need for reassurance or missing her touch, or both, he clutched her hand in both of his, rubbing it with his thumb.

Eyes widening, she blushed before tugging it away and wiping it on her jeans. "I-I'll see you in a bit."

His teeth clicked when he managed to unstick his open jaw. "Yeah. Let me help you with carrying stuff."

"I can handle myself, Callan." She headed for the door, removing her zip hoodie and tying it around her waist. "See you later."

He opened his mouth, but nothing came out. He sighed and closed his eyes. Clearly, she was upset with him. How was he going to fix this?

REMY SILENTLY WALKED outside. She was grateful for the distance from Callan. Finally, she could ruminate without fear of interruption.

Things were different now. Well, why was he acting like they weren't? And that's what irked her the most; he was the one who had been a jerk. How could he pretend as if nothing had happened?

Alia had been right about him, and Remy wondered why she felt so agitated when she had told herself there was no reason to be. There were no strings attached between them. But Remy couldn't let go of his words. He had avoided her the whole week.

And now that they were at work, even when it was just the two of them, he was acting as if nothing was wrong. Maybe he didn't think any-thing *was* wrong. Perhaps he didn't even know that his actions had hurt her.

Maybe he didn't care. Maybe he wasn't just a no-strings-attached guy. He was an actual, heartless person. She cursed herself internally for being so sensitive.

"Remy?"

She turned back to see the short, bald director standing there.

"Hey, Sam. What's up?" She tried to sound nonchalant. Sam stood next to her on the railing and lit a cigarette.

"How do you know that project manager?" he asked, puffing out smoke.

"He lives in the apartment next to mine," she replied, an unintentional edge in her tone, he noticed and raised his eyebrows.

"He's hot. Is he single?"

Remy giggled. "Yeah, he's single. But he's a jerk."

"Who cares?" Sam rolled his eyes in an exaggerated manner, his tone light. "Look at that scrumptious ass."

"I don't think he's into men, Sam. But you're too good for him." Remy shook her head and sighed. "Anyway, I should head back inside."

"Okay." Sam took another drag and waved at her. "Hey, Remy."

"Yeah?" She turned to him.

"You're too good for him, too."

"Okay." She chuckled. "Thanks."

She was barely inside when she bumped into a manly chest. She looked up to see Callan standing there. She was going to move past him and keep walking, but he stepped in front of her again.

"I need to talk to you," he said, his jaw determined.

"I have nothing to say."

"Then just listen."

Remy looked up at him and folded her arms hesitantly.

He exhaled loudly and massaged his temples.

"I shouldn't have talked to you like that."

"Yeah, you shouldn't have," she agreed.

"I won't do it again." He scratched his neck. "I just get defensive easily, I guess."

"There won't be an again, Callan." She bit her lip. "I can't do this. I know there's no commitment, but I can't do something like this when there's no mutual respect."

"I'm sorry I made you feel that way." He gulped; he was obviously not used to apologizing. But he was still doing it. "The thing is, we started off too fast. Maybe we should sit and talk? Get things out of the way. I won't pursue you anymore if your answer is still the same at the end of it."

Remy contemplated his offer for a while.

"Okay," she answered, still a bit tentative. "But I have to work now."

"Later, then. I'm leaving now, but come over after you're done with work? I'll make you dinner."

"Are you going to yell at me again if I compliment your cooking?" She raised an eyebrow.

"Will you punish me if I do?" He smirked. She couldn't help but chuckle. He smiled at her, but she couldn't place his expression. His eyes had a faraway look in them, and his smile seemed just a little bit sad.

CHAPTER 8
THE EXPECTED UNEXPECTED

Remy cut into the roasted chicken; her mouth looked like it was about to water. Callan couldn't help but be proud of his creation.

"Like what you see?" he grinned. "Tastes even better than it looks."

She took a bite after dipping it in gravy and hummed, "Just like you."

He chuckled, but looking at her with a look of pure bliss on her face as she closed her eyes and savored each bite, he couldn't help the blood that rushed to his groin.

He cleared his throat to interrupt his thoughts. She looked up questioningly.

He shook his head and encouraged her to eat.

"You called me here to talk." She stated as she swallowed her bite and went in for another one.

"Yeah, I figured we could just establish some ground rules if we're going to do this."

"Okay." She nodded. "No feelings would be a given, I guess."

"Well, yeah."

"Also, no snapping at each other." She glared at him.

"I said I was sorry." He threw up his hands again.

"Okay, so, is there something that you want to try?" She asked, pushing her food around.

He felt confused but curious. "For example?"

"Well," She ate two bites of the chicken in succession and then looked at him. "Do you mind being tied up?"

"Whoa!" He was caught off guard. "With ropes?"

"I don't know. Not immediately. It's just something that I've wanted to try out." Remy shrugged.

The next thing he knew, He was lying down on his bed, his shirt tied around his eyes. She didn't tie up his hands with ropes or anything. Not being able to see a thing, only feel. She slid his cock in and out of her mouth, hands tracing his balls. Making light whimpering and gagging noises as she held down his wrists with her hands and his hips bucked up, his tip hitting the back of her throat was the most exhilarating sexual experience he had ever had.

As they lay together later, and she asked him if that had been okay, and if he'd enjoyed it, he felt something shift in his perception of her. He wasn't sure if he liked it.

Things went smoothly from then on. He would go over to her place, or she would come over to his.

They would watch a movie, or he would cook dinner, and later, things would get heated between them. The sex was the best Callan had ever had, and it was mutually beneficial in other ways too.

Many times, he tried to teach Remy how to cook it. It ended disastrously, but he still had fun. In fact, he could not remember having more fun at any other time.

Things started changing more when Remy helped him finally unpack the billion boxes in his apartment and helped him set everything in place.

He was sure this wasn't how things usually happened in 'Friends with Benefits' situations. But when he had bought it up with Remy, she had just shrugged it off and said, "Well, we're friends too, right?" And that had been the end of it.

But slowly, Callan realized that he was getting attached; he wasn't only getting attached to her presence, but to her.

Fuck. He said to himself one night as he was going to sleep with her in his arms. She was snoring lightly and drooling and didn't look attractive at all, but he suddenly thought about how he wouldn't mind staying like that forever.

CHAPTER 9
LET'S START AGAIN

Remy swiped her phone to check the text she had just received.

Can you come over? I need to talk. It's kind of serious.

Her brain went into anxious mode. What did he want to talk about? Did he want to end things?

Did he figure out I was getting attached?

She bit her lip. She had wanted to tell him it wasn't fair to either of them. However, every time she worked up the courage to do it, they would get caught up in a heated position.

She rang his doorbell, and he opened it in a second.

"Come in."

"Is everything okay?" she asked as soon as she stepped into the kitchen.

"I quit my job," he announced.

"You what?" She was confused. Is this why he called her over? He looked anxious, so she set aside her questions and sat down. "Um. Is everything okay?"

"Yeah." He scratched the back of his head. "I've never really liked corporate. Or business. I quit my job. My parents disinherited me, but whatever."

"They disinherited you?" she yelled.

"Yeah." He sighed. "But I'm going to start working as a chef."

"Why did your parents disinherit you?" She was still confused. "They didn't want you working as a chef?"

"Yeah, it's not high-class enough for them, apparently."

"Callan, I'm glad you're opening up, but is there a reason you're telling me this?" She asked hesitantly.

She sat and listened as Callan told her everything. The parental pressure, the abuse, everything. She was shocked at how calmly he talked about it all. Like those things hadn't happened to him, but someone else. She felt a growing admiration for him in her heart. But also worry.

"I'm telling you all this because this is the reason why I snapped at you the other day." He looked up to lock eyes with her. "I don't want you to feel bad for me, but I want to be honest with you."

"I don't feel bad for you, Callan. Thanks for telling me." She shook her head.

"I also think we should stop sleeping together."

"What?" Remy asked, her heart sinking. She had expected this to happen sooner or later, but it still stung. "Okay. If that's what you want."

"Yeah." He looked down. "It's not fair to you. You deserve better."

Now she was really confused. What was he doing?

"What are you on about?" she asked, annoyed.

Callan sighed and met her eyes, giving her a sad smile.

"I have feelings for you, Remy."

"What?"

"Yeah, I don't think I can go on and end up getting hurt. But I'm not going to hold you back so..."

"Shut up."

"What?" He looked at her, confused. He seemed vulnerable, and his hands were trembling. She wanted to kiss him right then and there, but she held herself back.

"Can I kiss you?" She sighed, exasperated. She couldn't find the words, and she couldn't take it any longer.

"Please."

Their lips crushed together easily, moving so naturally. They'd gotten so used to the way the other kissed; they matched seamlessly.

They kissed and kissed. Remy pulled Callan forward and perched herself on the table, and then they kissed and kissed and kissed some more. But this was different. It was more romantic, the kind of kiss she wouldn't want to pull away from.

"Wait," Callan said, breaking away. "We should make this official."

"What are we, fifteen?" Remy scoffed and pulled him back with his shirt collar "Yeah, yeah. Be my boyfriend and whatever. Just put your tongue back in my mouth,"

Callan put a hand against her mouth.

"No, seriously, I don't want to half-ass this." He spoke earnestly. "I mean it."

Remy pushed away his hand so she could speak.

"Look, Callan, we know nothing is ever going to be perfect," she sighed. "If we have an issue, we'll talk it out. All I want is to be able to trust you."

"You can trust me, Remy." He gazed into her eyes. There was a promise in them. "And I'm going to kiss you now, but we're going to have this conversation again later. You're too horny to think straight right now."

"Wow, I'm proud of your growth, Mr. Price."

Callan kissed her for what felt like hours, and Remy loved every second of it.

They didn't even have sex that night, just kissed and enjoyed each other's presence.

Okay, that was a lie, they went three rounds. But there was a lot of kissing the whole time.

Thank You. Here Is A FREE Gift!
If You Could Please Leave This Book And The Free Book An Honest Review.
Click Here To Leave A Review[1]

---

1. https://www.amazon.com/review/create-re-

view/?ie=UTF8&channel=glance-detail&asin=B086NPRLGH

Sensual Investments: The Intern (Book One)
<<<Download For FREE Here>>>[2]

Sensual Investments: The Executive (Book Two)
Download Here[3]

---

3. https://buy.bookfunnel.com/5pkda664z6

LEAVE ME A REVIEW!

If you enjoyed this book or found it useful, please take a moment to leave a review on Amazon!

Click Here To Leave A Review[1]

Thank you for your support!

If you sign up for my newsletter you will receive my next book for free!

Signup Here!

Click Here To Sign Up To Paulina's Sexy Newsletter[2]

Interested in other books like this one?

<<<See Below>>>

---

1. https://www.amazon.com/review/create-re-view/?ie=UTF8&channel=glance-detail&asin=B086WFY-WHH

2. https://BookHip.com/LVRGWC

Also By Paulina Young

Booking the Babysitter: A Couple's Guilty Pleasure

Download Here[1]

---

1. https://buy.bookfunnel.com/z5tfll2v0p

A Politician's Dark Secret

Download Here[2]

Naughty Nights with the Nanny: Babysitter Turned Sex Slave

Download Here[3]

---

3. https://buy.bookfunnel.com/36dmo200ny

Tied in Thailand: Bound for the Beach and Bondage

Download Here[4]

About the Author

Paulina Young is an emerging LGBTQ+ Erotica and Steamy Romance Author who is on a mission to spread positive vibes and love to as many people as possible. Hailing from the dangerous streets of south Chicago, she eventually escaped the mayhem through her storytelling and by venturing out to the suburbs. In addition to her passion for crafting romance-driven plots, she was crowned Local South Chicago Writers Club Author of the Year. Her various short story achievements also earned her a feature in the Chicago Tribune.

When she isn't penning steamy scenes, you can find this free-spirited lover painting beautiful landscapes, hiking around local trails, sailing, or dancing her heart out.

If Paulina had to pick one superpower, it would have to be X-ray vision (for obvious reasons). As for her personal motto: "Don't give up and keep working hard to achieve your goals."

Read more at https://www.amazon.com/-/e/B085TQP6V3.